Helping in Class

TAKING CIVIC ACTION

Reggie Harper

CIVICS FOR THE REAL WORLD™

Rosen Classroom™

Helping in class is a nice thing to do. How do you help in class?

Painting is lots of fun. You can help wash the paintbrushes.

Your friend needs help reading. You can read books with them.

Are you good at math?

You can help your friend.

Using a computer can be hard. Show your friend how to do it.

Don't talk during class.

This helps everyone learn!

WORDS TO KNOW

book

computer

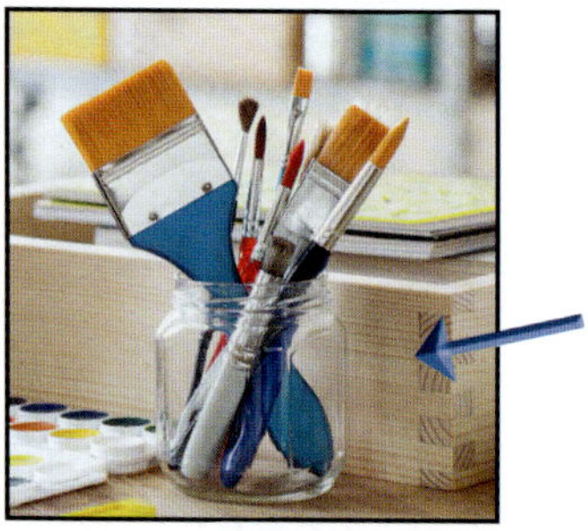

paintbrush